'Of Course You Can Meet The Queen!'

by Richard Penny

Pictures by Chris Baker

Ever since the Duke of Gloucester came to visit my school,
I've been dreaming of meeting the Queen of England.
One day, not so long after the Duke's visit, I told a friend.
'You can't meet the Queen!' she said.

When I got home, I sat down next to Daddy.

'Daddy?' I said.

'Yes, darling girl?' he replied.

'Well, I was wondering whether I might be able to meet the Queen.'

He wasn't ready for that, and spilt some tea over his shirt.

'Of course you can meet the Queen!' he said.

'I'll write Her Majesty a letter and ask very nicely.'

'Really? Would you?' I said, shaking with excitement.

After a few weeks, we received a reply from Buckingham Palace.
'It's not the best news we've ever had, but at least we tried,' he said.
I didn't know what to say, so I just huffed and wandered off.

Next day, Daddy had what he calls a 'brainwave'.

'How about we go to Buckingham Palace and wait at the gates,' he said.

'We'll go every Saturday and Sunday from sunrise to sunset.

The Queen is sure to meet you after a while.'

I jumped into his arms. 'When do we start?' I asked.

'It's Saturday tomorrow,' he said, with a wink.

Very early next morning, Mummy and I went downstairs
while Daddy packed a few things in his bag.
I quizzed Mummy about the Queen while she made some
lovely sandwiches and drinks for us, and then it was time
to set off and catch the bus into London.

When we arrived, I couldn't believe how big and beautiful the palace was.

Daddy saw a nice area in front of the gates, so we set out a blanket and waited.

The guard gave us a funny look after a while, but we weren't bothered.

We would wait, and that was that.

We played a few games and had some lunch.

Then I did some drawing while Daddy read a book.

As the sun was setting, we started to pack up our things.

'Do you think the Queen knows that we're here?' I asked.

Daddy held up the 'brainwave' finger, and approached the guard.

'Would you kindly inform Her Majesty that my daughter and I will wait here every weekend until such a time that Her Majesty wishes to see us?'

I saw the guard nod ever so slightly.

Daddy came back. 'Affirmative,' he said.

On Sunday morning, Daddy woke me up, but I was dreaming about fairies.
'Do you want to meet the Queen?' he whispered, and my eyes popped open.

Again, we set up our little place in front of the gates next to the guard.
Daddy had brought some great felt-tip pens.
He gave me a photograph of the Queen and asked if I would draw
a special picture of the great lady.

By lunchtime, the guard that Daddy had spoken to came on duty.
He gave me a nice smile when I looked up at him.
By the time the sun had set, I felt very tired.
We'd played so much I-spy that there was nothing left to guess.
'Darling?' said Daddy. 'Would you ask the guard if he might take your picture
and pass it on to the Queen?'
I did so, and the guard took the piece of paper and put it in a pocket very quickly.
He looked down and smiled at me.

Once we'd packed up our things, we thanked the guard and caught the bus home.

At school, I told my friends what I'd been doing over the weekend.

'The Queen doesn't have time to see you!' they said. 'Your Dad must be mad!'

I got home and told Daddy.

'If you don't have a dream, how can you make a dream come true?' he said,
and it made perfect sense.

On Saturday morning, we arrived at Buckingham Palace
and set out our place.

Mummy came to visit us with my little sister at lunchtime
and we ate some lovely food together.

In the afternoon, Mummy took my sister into St James' Park
to look at the birds and play.

It was a sunny day and I so wanted to join them,
but I knew I had to stay with Daddy.

Just as the sun was setting, Mummy and my sister came back
and we all caught the bus home.

On Sunday morning, we set up as usual outside the palace
but I couldn't help thinking of all the things I could have been doing
on a normal Sunday.
The day passed very slowly.
When the sun finally set, we packed up and went home on the bus.
'Don't be sad, darling,' said Daddy. 'Next weekend will be different.'

So, on Saturday morning, we arrived at the palace
to set up our little place by the gates.
Daddy had brought a big bag of colourful building blocks.
By lunchtime, we'd made a beautiful castle.

In the afternoon, a lot of people arrived with banners.

They were all shouting about something.

I asked Daddy what the fuss was about.

'These people are all fighting for something they believe in,

and they've come to tell the Queen,' he said.

'Can the Queen help them?' I asked.

'Of course, darling,' he replied. 'That's why they're here, like us,

only for a different reason.'

After a while, the police came to calm things down.

An angry man with a red face walked past and knocked down my castle.

'That's what I think of the Queen!' he shouted.

'Oh, well,' said Daddy as we gathered up the blocks.

'At least it's been an eventful day.'

The sun set soon after, so we packed away our things and caught the bus home.

That night, I had a wonderful dream about the Queen.

I couldn't remember much about it but on Sunday morning,

I was ready before Daddy.

'I was there, with the Queen in my dream!' I told him.

'It's all for a reason, darling,' he said.

As usual, we placed our blanket at our spot by the gates.

In the morning, Daddy read a lovely story about a prince and his princess.

Mummy came with my little sister at lunchtime and we played together,

but then it started to rain.

'She'll catch a cold,' said Mummy to Daddy as they left to go home.

'It won't rain for long,' he replied. 'Besides, fortune favours the brave.'

It poured down all afternoon.

We had our waterproofs so we just stood there by the gates

looking like soggy penguins.

With all the dark clouds and rain,

we started to wonder if the sun had already set.

Then the streetlights came on.

'Would you like to go now, darling?' asked Daddy.

'Let's just wait a little longer,' I said.

I don't know what made me say that, but it just came out.

Moments later, I noticed a silhouette appear in one of the windows of the palace.

But then the silhouette disappeared and my heart sank.

The sky was almost pitch black and the rain was heavy.
In the distance, I noticed that the guard we'd befriended
was marching towards us, and my heart began to race with excitement.

When he walked past us, I realised that he had only come
to relieve the guard on duty.
The other guard left, and my hopes seemed to go with him.

But then, something magical happened.

Without turning to face us, the guard spoke out.

'Please go through the gates and proceed to the main entrance of the palace,' he said.

I jumped for joy!

While Daddy picked up our things, I went over to the guard and looked up at him.

'Thank you very much, sir,' I said.

As we approached the entrance to the palace,
I felt excited and scared at the same time.
A man in a black suit met us and we were shown in.
'Follow me, please,' he said.

It was quite dark inside.

As we walked through an enormous hall,

I could just make out all the paintings on the walls.

The rooms we walked through seemed to get smaller and smaller,

then we were shown up some stairs.

Suddenly, we stopped at a door.

Our guide knocked three times and we could hear a voice from inside.

'Come in,' the voice said.

I shook with excitement as we entered.

There was a figure over by the window.

'Your Majesty,' said the usher, and the Queen turned to face us.

'Thank you,' said the Queen, and he left.

The Queen welcomed us in and held out a hand for us

to sit at a table with three sets of cutlery.

Daddy stood behind me as I curtseyed.

'Would you like to join me for supper?' said the Queen. 'You must be starving.'

'Oh yes, please, Your Majesty,' I said.

'I received the lovely picture you gave to the guard,' said the Queen,

pointing to the mantelpiece.

And there it was.

My heart was filled with joy and I thanked Her Majesty for putting it there.

'Philip loves it,' said the Queen.

As we went to sit down, a man in a white suit entered with a silver trolley.
'Sausages with roast potatoes, vegetables and gravy,'
announced the man before leaving.

'Yippee!' I said. 'My favourite.'

The Queen smiled at me just as my grandmother does.
We all ate our food and it was delicious.

After supper, the Queen gave me a silver necklace and kissed me on the cheek.

'That's for all your trouble,' said the Queen.

'Oh, it was no trouble at all, Your Majesty,' I replied, holding back tears.

The usher arrived to take us downstairs, so we said goodbye

and thanked the Queen for inviting us.

Daddy picked up our things that he'd left by the entrance
and we walked back to the gates.
We took one last look at the palace and there was the Queen,
waving goodbye from the balcony.
We waved back.

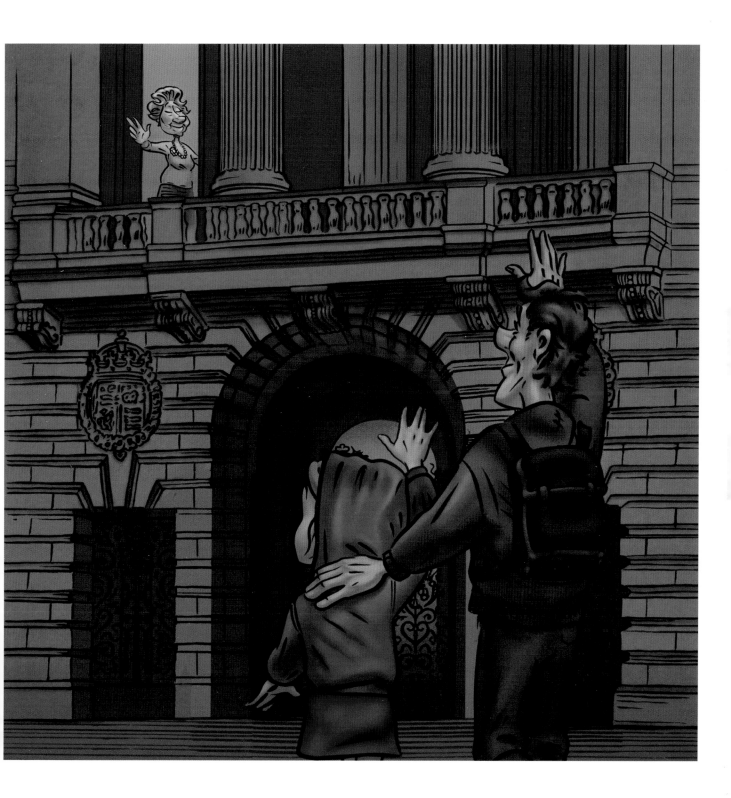

At the gates, I approached the guard and blew a kiss to him.

He smiled down at me for a moment.

'Thank you again, sir,' I said. 'I'll never forget this day for as long as I live.'

When we got home, Mummy just couldn't believe it,

but when I showed her the silver necklace, she held me and kissed me.

'Well done, darling,' she said with a little tear in her eye. 'Your dream came true!'

The next day, I went to school and told my friends, but no one believed me.
'Don't fib,' they all said. 'The Queen doesn't eat sausages.'
'Oh yes, Her Majesty does,' I said.

First published in the UK
in 2011 by
Catchy Monkey books
1 Acacia Avenue
Woking, Surrey
GU22 0BE

catchymonkey.org

ISBN: 978-0-9567811-0-9
Copyright © Richard Penny

Printed in the UK
by Williams Press

50% of all profits from this edition will go to the children's charity, Railway Children